BIBLE VISUALS international

Helping Children See Jesus

ISBN: 978-1-64104-115-7

No Darkness At All
*An adaptation of Star of Light
by Patricia St. John*

Adapted by: Rose-Mae Carvin
Illustrators: Frances H. Hertzler, Linda McInturff
Computer Graphic Artists: Ed Olson, Jonathan Ober, Yuko Willoughby
Page Layout: Patricia Pope

© 2020 Bible Visuals International,
PO Box 153, Akron, PA 17501-0153
Phone: (717) 859-1131
www.biblevisuals.org

Published by Scripture Union in England and used by arrangement with them.
© 1953 by Patricia St. John
Scripture Union USA: PO Box 987 #1, Valley Forge, PA 19482
CANADA: 1885 Clements Road Unit 226, Pickering ON L1W 3V4 All rights reserved.

RELATED ITEMS

To access related items (such as activities, memory verse posters and translated texts) please visit our web store at www.biblevisuals.org and enter 5340 at the top right of the web page. You may need to reduce the zoom setting to get the search box.

FREE TEXT DOWNLOAD

To obtain a FREE printable copy of the teaching text (PDF format) please scroll down and select Extra–PDF Teacher Text Download to place in your shopping cart. When checking out, use coupon code XTACSV17 at checkout. Under Product Format select English and click on Apply Coupon for the discount. Other languages are available at an additional cost.

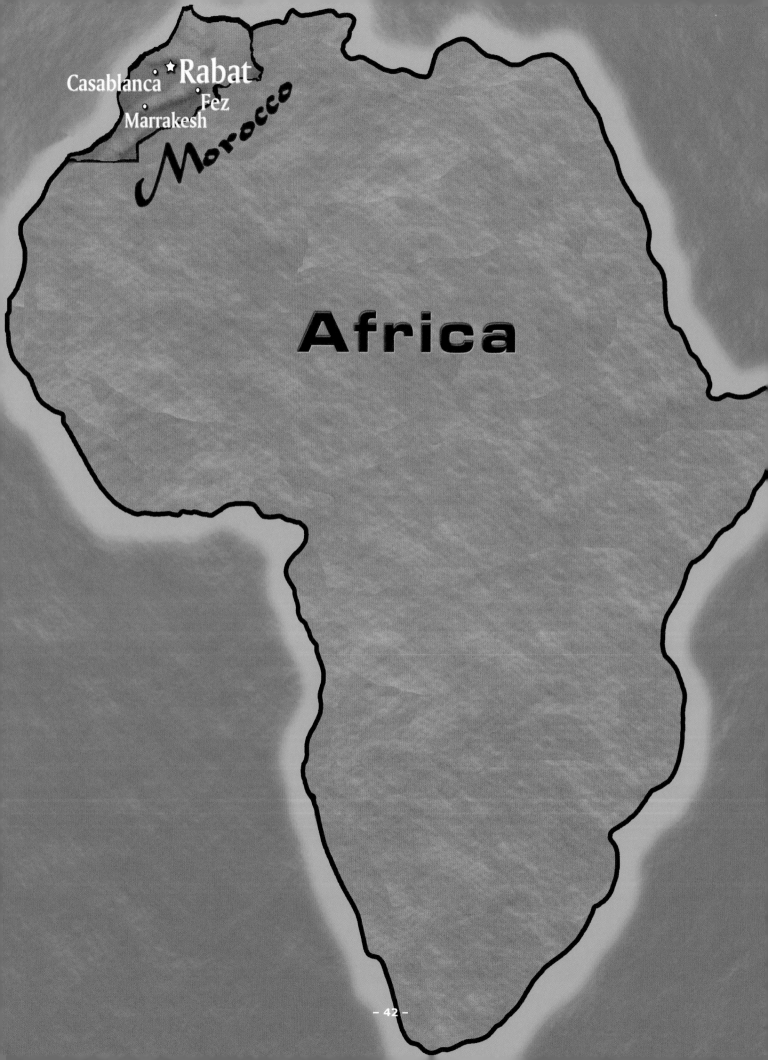

Casablanca • ★ **Rabat**

• **Fez**

• **Marrakesh**

Morocco

Africa

This then is the message which we have heard of Him, and declare unto you, that God is light, and in Him is no darkness at all.

1 John 1:5

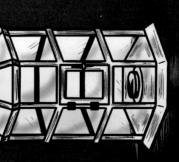

Then spake Jesus again unto them, saying, "I am the Light of the world; he that followeth Me shall not walk in darkness, but shall have the Light of life."

John 8:12

– 44 –

NOTE TO THE TEACHER

You can teach this story with confidence, knowing that the author, Patricia St. John, served the Lord as a missionary nurse among the people of whom she writes. Throughout each chapter of this story, helpful information about Morocco is set apart in *Teacher, Did you know . . .* boxes.

If you need correlated Bible teaching material, we suggest *Bible Lessons to Light the Way*. The lessons are illustrated in color and are a perfect supplement to this story. Also available is a related, visualized Gospel hymn, "The Light of the World Is Jesus". These may be purchased from Bible Visuals International. Reproducible Scripture memory verse tokens are included in this volume.

This then is the message which we have heard of Him and declare unto you, that God is light, and in Him is no darkness at all (1 John 1:5).

The *aim* of the lesson: To teach that there is only one true God and that the only way to worship Him is through the Lord Jesus Christ.

Pronunciations

Place slightly more emphasis on the last syllable in both instances.
Hamid is pronounced Ha (as in ha ha) and mid (as in midway).
Kinza is pronounced Kin (as keen) and za (as zah).

Glossary

This is a list of unfamiliar words used in this volume.

Allah	Islam's god	Muslim	Follower of Islam
Muhammad	Founder of Islam	Mosque	Building where Muslims pray
Qur'an	Sacred scriptures of Islam	Paradise	Where good Muslims are said to go after death
Islam	Religion based on Qur'an		

Show Map

Morocco lies in the northwestern corner of the continent of Africa between Algeria (on the northeast) and Mauritania (in the south). The country's northwest border rolls down to the Atlantic Ocean and the Mediterranean Sea. The Sahara Desert covers much of southwestern Morocco.

Arab Muslims took Morocco by force over 1,300 years ago. Now, to be Moroccan is to be Muslim. Muslims worship one whom they call *Allah*. They say that Allah had many prophets, but the greatest was Muhammad. A Muslim says often, "There is no god but Allah, and Muhammad is his prophet."

Muslims bow in prayer to Allah. They pray before the graves of the leaders who came after Muhammad, believing they are saints and have power to heal. Muslims bow and pray five times every 24 hours. They do not forget to pray, for the call to prayer is announced over a loudspeaker system from the highest part of the mosque (building where Muslims worship).

Moroccans need to hear the Word of God. They must hear of the true and living God and of His Son, the Lord Jesus Christ. Who will tell them?

In a village, where the Rif Mountains rise above the town, we meet a Muslim boy, Hamid, and our adventure begins.

Show Illustration #1

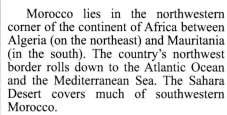

Hamid was only 11 years old, but he had been well trained to take care of goats. Had he not been doing so for two years and more–ever since his father had died and his mother had married his wicked stepfather?

As Hamid sat and watched his goats, he thought of the days when his own father had been alive. Everything had been much happier then. Now he knew his stepfather hated him, and worse still, his stepfather hated Hamid's sweet little baby sister.

Hamid could stand the beatings if only his little sister Kinza were treated better. Hamid knew his mother was very unhappy. He thought it had something to do with Kinza. His young heart ached to see his mother so sad.

To make things worse, Hamid's stepfather had another wife. She was very old and very mean, and she hated Hamid's mother

and the children. *Perhaps it is because she has no children of her own,* Hamid reasoned.

Two of the young goats took advantage of Hamid's daydreaming and scurried over to a patch of wheat. They skipped about in every direction, giving merry little bleats as they leaped high in the air. Finally Hamid noticed. He hurried to round them up.

Show Illustration #2

It was then that Hamid saw one of his boy friends running down the hillside toward him. The boy's scanty rags seemed to be having a hard time keeping up with him. *Something is wrong,* Hamid thought. As soon as the boy was within hearing distance Hamid shouted, "What's wrong? Have you brought bad news?"

"No, no," the boy panted. "It is just that your mother wants you right away. She wants you to hurry and meet her at the well. I am to mind the goats for you."

Hamid handed the boy a big stick to use in keeping the goats in order. Without a word, Hamid turned and hurried up the steep path which led from the valley to his home and the well on the side of the mountain.

As he climbed, Hamid thought about his mother and how worried she had seemed for a long time. Hamid felt quite certain that her sadness had something to do with his little sister, Kinza. He had noticed how carefully his mother tried to keep Kinza out of sight of her husband and the old wife. Hamid quickened his steps.

Hamid found his mother waiting for him at the well. She had two empty buckets in her hands and little Kinza tied to her back with a piece of cloth.

"Hurry, Hamid," his mother whispered. "Hide these buckets quickly in the bushes and come with me. We must hurry before the old wife sends someone to look for me. She thinks I have come only for water."

Without a word Hamid followed his mother. When they were out of sight of the little one-room hut which was their home, Hamid's mother untied the cloth and laid Kinza in her lap.

Show Illustration #3

"Look closely at your little sister, Hamid. Show her some flowers. Smile at her."

Hamid did as his mother commanded. Kinza showed no signs of pleasure. With fear in his heart, Hamid looked more closely at her, into her eyes. He passed his hand before her face. She did not blink.

"She is blind," he whispered.

"Yes, she is blind."

They sat still for a moment. Neither spoke.

Then Hamid's mother said, "Come, my son. We must hurry. I want you to go with me to the saint's tomb. I shall pray for Kinza."

Climbing higher up the mountain, Hamid and his mother came to a small cave, shaded by a bush. On the bush, dirty little pieces of paper were tied. Each told that another had come there to pray and had fastened his or her bit of paper to the bush.

Hamid's mother laid Kinza at the mouth of the cave. She bowed low many times, calling on Allah and the prophet Muhammad to heal her baby. Then she looked eagerly into Kinza's face. The child still could not see!

Bitterly disappointed, Hamid and his mother hurried down just as the sun was setting behind the mountain. Kinza could

not see. *Perhaps Allah does not care that she is blind,* Hamid thought, *and so the saint will do nothing to helOr perhaps baby girls are beneath his notice.*

How dreadful, Hamid thought, *that little Kinza should never see the light!* She was always in darkness. Hamid hated darkness. He was afraid of the evil spirits which, he had been taught, wandered about in darkness. How he longed for a place where there was no darkness at all. Yet he did not know that he was in much worse darkness than the darkness of night. He was in *spiritual* darkness–a darkness of being separated from God.

Show Illustration #4

He was in that darkness because he had never been told of the Lord Jesus, who is the Light of life.

Back at the well, Hamid filled his mother's buckets with water and gave them to her. As she turned and walked wearily to the hut, Hamid turned and went slowly down the path and to his goats. He found them huddled against the legs of his friend. Their eyes gleamed like green lanterns in the twilight.

Handing his friend a piece of dark bread as payment for watching the goats, Hamid herded them up the path to the village.

He passed several dark huts in the village before he came to his own. But before he had reached it he heard a loud, angry voice. It was the old wife scolding his mother. Someone had seen Hamid and his mother go to the saint's tomb. The old woman knew!

"Wicked, deceitful, lazy one!" she shouted. "Give me that child! Let me see for myself why you hide her and sneak away with her to the tomb."

Snatching the little girl away from her mother, the old wife carried her to the light. She felt all over the baby's body, to see if it might be crippled. She stared into Kinza's sweet little face.

Show Illustration #5

Then she knew. She laughed an ugly, cackling laugh which made Kinza cry. "Just wait until I tell the master that Kinza is blind," she cried, as she threw Kinza into the mother's arms.

Yet when the husband came home, things did not happen in just the way the old woman and the young wife had expected.

He did not speak to his wives, nor to Hamid, as he stooped to enter the low door—the only opening to the one-room hut. Instead, he simply motioned for food to be placed before him.

Show Illustration #6

Hamid's mother placed one bowl of hot food on the low table at which her husband sat cross-legged on the floor. She handed him a large piece of black bread. To the rest of the family she handed smaller pieces, and together they dipped in the single bowl. As they dipped they said, "In the name of Allah." This they said in order to keep evil spirits away.

As soon as the meal was over, the old wife grabbed up Kinza and carried her to the stepfather. Handing him a lighted candle, she exclaimed, "Look closely!"

With surprise the stepfather saw that Kinza was indeed blind. Yet instead of shouting with rage and beating the young wife and her children, he sat quietly for a time, smoking his hookah (a long, thin pipe). Then he said, "Blind children can be very profitable. Keep the baby carefully. She may bring us much money."

"But how?" the trembling young mother asked.

"By begging. Not that we can beg with her. We are honorable people. But I know a beggar who will be glad to hire her to sit with him on market days. People are sorry for blind children!"

Show Illustration #7

And so it was that wee Kinza, scarcely two years old, was rented out to a filthy blind man who took her one day a week when the market came to town.

It was Hamid's duty to carry her on his back to the beggar as soon as she had finished her breakfast of sweet, black coffee. At the end of the day Hamid

collected the money and carried the tired little girl back home. Hamid grew to love his sister more and more. And Kinza dearly loved her brother.

Hamid knew Kinza hated the market with all the noise and dust that made her sneeze, the flies that crawled over her face, and the fleas that bit her legs. And so if he could beg or steal a little money during the week, he would always buy Kinza a lump of sticky green candy on market day. After a few secret licks for himself he would give the candy to Kinza just as he left her with the beggar.

Hamid was always back before it was time for Kinza to go home. He stood outside the market and kept his eyes on the mosque (church). When the priest appeared in the high tower and shouted to tell the people it was four o'clock and time for prayer, Hamid dashed over to where little Kinza sat, almost asleeHamid kissed the old beggar's hand, instead of saying "Hello," as we do. Then he snatched up Kinza in his arms.

He always tried to bring her a leathery ring of fried dough to eat, for Hamid knew she would have had only water and dark bread. She might have had a squashed plum–if she had collected a lot of money that morning.

How glad Hamid was to take his little sister away from the old beggar whose filthy clothing was falling to pieces! He could not bear to think of his little sister sitting so close to the wicked man for a whole day at a time.

Late one night as Hamid lay sleeping on the low mattress along the wall of the one-room home, he awoke suddenly. The grown-ups were still sitting around the dead charcoal fire, talking.

Show Illustration #8

Hamid shivered. He did not shiver so much from the cold. He shivered with fear because of what he heard coming from his stepfather's lips.

"It is the only offer we shall ever get for her. The beggar is moving away. He will take her and she will be taken care of."

Kinza's mother cried, "She will die– she is so little and so weak."

Hamid wanted to rush to his mother's side and declare, "They shall not sell our Kinza." But he did not dare to move.

"A blind child is better dead," he heard the old wife say.

Hamid waited until he heard the deep breathing of the old wife and the husband. Then he crept softly, feeling his way in the darkness, to where his mother sat by the dead fire.

"It won't happen, Mother," he whispered. "I won't let her go."

We all feel sorry for Hamid, and especially for little Kinza. We wish that we might indeed tell them to turn to the true God who loves little children.

Our God is the only true God. God loved us so much He sent the Lord Jesus all the way from Heaven, where He was rich, to our earth, where He was poor. Why did the Lord Jesus come? So He could die upon the cross for our sins.

We can serve the true God only if we belong to Him. And we can belong to Him only by receiving the Lord Jesus as our Saviour. God's Word, the Bible, tells us this. (Use John 3:16.)

But Hamid knew only about the Qur'an, which is the Muslim holy book. The Qur'an does not tell the truth about the Lord Jesus. And so, unless someone tells Hamid why the Lord Jesus died on the cross, he will never know.

We *do* know. Would you like to invite the Saviour, the Lord Jesus Christ, to come into your heart and forgive your sin?

Would you like to do this today?

Teacher, Did you know . . .

RELIGION:

Hamid is a Muslim, a follower of the religion called Islam. Muslims do not know they need a Redeemer or Saviour. They believe that by obeying the *Five Pillars*, or five main beliefs of Islam, perhaps their good works will be enough so hopefully at death Allah will allow them into Paradise. The *Five Pillars* are:

1. Shahada: Reciting the Creed: "There is no God but Allah and Muhammad is his prophet." To become a convert to Islam, you must recite this belief publicly.
2. Salat: Reciting prayers five specified times every day.
3. Zakat: Giving 2½ cents of every dollar to the poor (technically out of their wealth after expenses).
4. Swam: Fasting during daylight hours during the month of Ramadan.
5. Hajj: Taking a once-in-their-lifetime journey to Mecca, Islam's most important site.

To be Moroccan is to be Muslim. Hamid sincerely believes the Qur'an (written by Muhammad 500+ years after the Bible). He may have been told since he was little that the Bible is inferior to the Qur'an and is corrupted. He may have also heard a teacher of the Qur'an say, "the Injeel (or Gospel of Jesus) has been lost, and only the Qur'an restores God's truth to mankind." (*Teacher:* Yet the Qur'an supports the fact that the Torah, Psalms and Gospel of Jesus were given by God!) Whenever Hamid's parents speak or write the founder of Islam's name, Muhammad, they respectfully add these words, "Peace be upon him," or

the initials PBUH after his name.

Hamid has never read the Bible. But he may have heard stories passed down from older people who quoted the Qur'an about Moses, Abraham, and Jesus. Islam teaches that "Jesus must have been very blest by Allah (god of Islam) to do miracles. But it is wrong to say Jesus is God." Boys like Hamid, if they have heard this, may believe that Jesus was a good teacher for Allah, but that Muhammad was Allah's last, most important messenger. Muslims don't believe Jesus died on the cross for sins, but that Judas was put on the cross and died in Jesus's place.

Many *Imams* (religious leaders) require Muslim children to memorize many *surahs* (chapter and verses) of the Qur'an. And every day, five times a day, boys like Hamid stop their activities to pray when the *Muezzin* announces the Muslim call to prayer from the minaret, a high tower in a corner of the Mosque. "Allah akbar, Allah, akbar" is heard booming out from the loudspeakers. (This call may differ in non-Arabic-speaking countries.) Muslims face east toward Mecca. Muslims use various positions for prayer and recite prayers they have learned. Muslims sometimes travel to the tombs of Muslim "saints" (leaders after Muhammad) to seek protection from the *jinn* (spirits whom they believe roam in the dark and bring great harm). *Jinn* are the basis for Hamid's fear of the night. Yet Hamid is living in "darkness" far greater than the darkness of nighttime. He does not know the God of the Bible who loves him.

Chapter 2

The *aim* of the lesson: To show that children everywhere are of special concern to God. He wants them to come to Him *today*.

Teacher, Did you know . . .

MOROCCAN CURRENCY: Dirhams

Equivalencies to US dollar:

US $10	=	1.15 Dirhams
US $20	=	2.30 Dirhams
US $1,000	=	115 Dirhams

Hamid could not sleep after he heard his stepfather's plan to sell Kinza outright to the filthy beggar. The darkness of the night seemed to press hard in the little hut. How Hamid hated it! *At least,* thought Hamid, *Kinza will never be afraid of the dark as I am, for she has never seen light.*

Hamid seemed to see the wicked face of the beggar beside the sweet face of his little sister. He knew Kinza would not live long if she belonged to the beggar. He would surely mistreat her.

And so Hamid lay awake, shivering and trying to find a way to save his little sister. If only Hamid could have known, as we do, about the Lord Jesus who could keep Kinza safe.

Just before Hamid finally fell into a troubled sleep, he heard his mother moaning softly, "Little daughter, little daughter!" He turned his face to the wall.

Early the next morning Hamid was awakened by a kick from his stepfather. "Wake up, you lazy creature. It's time you had the goats out."

Hamid rolled off his mattress, feeling as though he had not gone to bed at all. He washed his face and hands in a bucket and began his breakfast of bread and sweet coffee. He did not need to dress, for he never undressed to go to bed.

As he ate, Hamid noticed his mother staring hard at him. He returned her gaze. She raised her eyebrows a little and gave a slight nod. Hamid knew she wanted to talk to him as soon as possible.

Hamid hurried out of the hut. He sought out his friend and, with a crust of bread saved from his breakfast, bribed him to watch the goats. Then he crept back to hide behind a hedge and watch for his mother.

Soon he saw her go to the barn. Keeping himself hidden from the hut, Hamid slipped inside the barn and sat beside his mother. She sat cross-legged turning the heavy wheel to crush the corn.

Show Illustration #9

Hamid laid his hand on his mother's arm. "Have you thought of a way to save Kinza?" he asked.

Turning to her son, Hamid's mother looked at him carefully. She saw a thin little boy only 11 years old; but she knew he was tough and wiry. More than that, she knew how much he loved his little sister.

"Yes, my son, I have thought of a way. *You* shall save Kinza."

"I? But how? I lay awake most of the night trying to think of a way and could not. How can I save her?"

"Listen," said his mother, turning from the grindstone and laying her hands on his knees.

Hamid's eyes never left his mother's face as she spoke; and he never forgot her whispered words.

"When you were a baby your father took me to visit a tomb across the mountain. After we had visited the tomb, your father wanted to go on twenty more miles in order to see the market and trade a little.

"We walked from sunrise to sunset. The sun was hot on our heads and trucks passing by stirred up the dust which almost choked us. When we reached the town, my feet were cut and blistered and you were crying with fever.

"I washed you in one of the fountains running in the street, then we found a place to sleep in the yard of the inn. But the next morning, you were very sick with fever.

"I sat there and held you when your father went off to market. I tried to keep you out of the sun, and kept brushing the flies away. Then a woman of the town came and spoke to me. 'Is your baby sick?' she asked.

" 'Yes, he has fever,' I replied.

" 'Come quick,' the woman said. 'There is just time enough to get you to the home of the English nurse. She will give you medicine for your baby.'

" 'I have no money,' I said. 'Besides, the English are rich and live in fine houses. She will not receive me.'

" 'But she lives in one of our houses,' the woman said. 'She helps the poor, in the name of One she calls the Lord Jesus Christ. I think it is her Saint.' "

Hamid listened, wondering why he had never heard this before.

"The woman led me down a narrow, back street to a house with an open door. There were poor people coming out of that door–poor people with babies tied on their backs. Some carried bottles of medicine and none seemed to be afraid.

"We were just in time. The nurse was still there. She was tall, Hamid, and her hair and eyes were light. I had never seen anyone like her before. She took you in her arms as though she loved you. The medicine she gave me to give you made you well, Hamid."

Hamid thought, *Surely she does not expect me to take Kinza to the English nurse. That would be impossible.*

Show Illustration #10

"None of this I shall ever forget, my son," Hamid's mother continued. "Nor shall I ever forget the beautiful picture I saw on the wall in the nurse's home. I looked at it closely when she went to get medicine for you. The picture was of a Man with a very kind face. He was holding a little child in his arms. Other little children clung to His robe and looked up at Him, with no fear in their faces. I asked the nurse who the Man in the picture was. She said His name was the Lord Jesus Christ; that God had sent Him to make it possible for people everywhere to get to Heaven.

"She told me how the Man in the picture had healed the sick, how He loved everyone–rich and poor, grown-ups and children. I cannot remember all that she said. But I know she loved the Man in the picture, and that is why she, too, is kind to the sick and poor."

Drawing him close to her side, Hamid's mother said, "Son, I think for the sake of the Man in the picture, the English nurse would shelter Kinza. And so you, my son, must take Kinza to her."

Hamid was trembling. "But how, Mother? How can I do this? How shall I know the way? I'd be afraid of the dark nights."

Carefully, Hamid's mother explained to him how to take the safest way over the mountain trail, and how to follow the river in the next valley. "Perhaps you may get a ride in a truck when you are closer to the town," she said. "If not, you must walk, and Allah be with you."

* * * * * * * * * * *

In spite of his fear, Hamid never thought of refusing to carry Kinza away as his mother had said he must do. He wanted with all his heart to keep his little sister away from the wicked stepfather and the dirty beggar. But he was afraid he might fail. Even so, he knew he would try when the time came.

His mother sent him to care for the goats. Over and over again Hamid repeated the instructions his mother had given him.

That night as he lay on his hard mattress he saw the moon rise as he watched through the low door. He waited until he was certain his stepfather and the old wife were asleeThen on perfectly silent feet, Hamid slipped through the doorway and out behind the grain shed.

The old dog rattled his chain. Quickly Hamid buried his face in the dog's mangy coat and patted his head. The dog must not bark and spoil everything.

Soon his mother silently appeared with Kinza in her arms. Without a word she bound the child to Hamid's strong, young back. Kinza stirred and then, laying her head on the shoulder she knew so well, slept soundly.

Show Illustration #11

Hamid's mother tied two loaves of bread on his other shoulder, took both his hands in hers, and kissed them. Hamid pressed his mother's fingers to his lips and clung to her for a moment. Then he turned and went out into the darkness through the gate. He was trying, oh, so hard, to be brave. If only he had known about the loving Father to whom he could have turned for help and protection. But he did not. If only Hamid could have sung with us, "Suffer the little children to come unto Me." If only he could have known about the loving Lord Jesus who longed to be his Saviour. But he did not know.

Show Illustration #12

The moon made some light on the path for a time. Soon, however, Hamid was walking through the shadows of the olive trees. Often he stumbled, jostling the baby on his back. Yet Hamid pushed on, trying not to mind the darkness.

When the sun arose, Hamid stopped for breakfast. He broke off two pieces from one loaf of bread.

Leading Kinza to a little stream which ran down the side of the path, he gave her water to drink from his cupped hands. He washed her as best he could and wished he had asked his mother for a quarter of the family comb so he could comb out her tangled hair. He did the best he could with his fingers.

The path climbed along the edge of the brook. Hamid's back ached, but he knew he must get a little farther on before the sun was really hot. From time to time he bathed his sore feet in the stream of water along which he walked.

Show Illustration #13

Finally Hamid could not take another steHis head ached. His back ached. He knew that he must stop or he might fall asleep on his feet. Crawling into a wheat field, Hamid lay down with his head resting on his arm and with Kinza curled up in the crook of his knee. Hamid was so tired that he did not notice how close the field was to a village. There both he and Kinza fell fast asleep.

But little Kinza did not sleep for long. She had slept most of the night, snuggled on her brother's back. Now she wanted her mother. Perhaps if she crawled towards the noise she heard she would find her mother. The noise was exactly the kind of noise her mother made when she ground corn. So away Kinza crawled.

Hamid would have indeed been frightened if he could have seen his little sister as she toddled toward the sound of the grinding mill, arms outstretched, crying, "Umm" (Mother)!

Her dress was torn and dirty and covered all over with straw. Her black curls were tangled and matted together. She seemed to be wearing a halo of straw about her head. But Hamid did not know. And so he slept on all through the day.

Just as the sun was going down over the mountain again, Hamid awoke. Where was Kinza? Frightened, he crept carefully through the field calling her name softly.

Then he saw her! She was sitting on a doorsteTo Hamid it seemed as if the whole village had come to see this strange, blind child who apparently lived alone in the wheat field.

Show Illustration #14

Hamid knew he must stay hidden until dark. Later, when he knew that Kinza was sleeping soundly and that the rest of the

strange family was also asleep, he slipped quietly inside the hut and quickly gathered Kinza up in his strong young arms.

With his heart thumping, and gasping for breath, Hamid hurried again on his mission. He knew his father probably had not missed him until this evening. But now that his father had missed him, he would surely try to find him and Kinza. And so he must travel only at night. On and on went the trying-to-be-brave boy, still hating the darkness.

Show Illustration #15

At one part of his journey, Hamid needed to cross an open road. It was just barely light, and he felt safe. But it was a mistake. Two soldiers on horseback, who had traveled at night to avoid the heat, saw the little figure with its burden. Hamid knew them. They were from his village.

One of the soldiers made a grab for Hamid. "This is the runaway boy our village is looking for!" he screamed.

Hamid ducked and bolted down the mountainside. His sudden movement startled the soldier's horse. It reared in the air and plunged forward.

Hamid jumped over thorns and roots, forgetting his sore back, not daring to look back. But the soldiers did not intend to drive their horses into the thorns and scrubs. They shrugged their shoulders and rode on. It was not their job to hunt for runaway boys. They would tell the police in the market.

Many days passed before Hamid reached his destination. He found friendly women along the way who helped him. They gave him and Kinza food and kept them hidden during the day. At night Hamid traveled on.

Show Illustration #16

Finally he reached the village and found the narrow street, exactly as his mother had described it to him. He reached the home of the English nurse. He saw many dirty little boys enter the open door.

Show Illustration #17

When he heard singing inside, Hamid crept closer. As he peeked through the door he saw the picture his mother had seen. He saw the lovely Lord Jesus with a child about Kinza's age in His arms and other little children looking up into His face.

Realizing that he had reached the end of his journey safely, Hamid walked a short distance to a rubbish heap where he sat down and gently shook Kinza until she was awake. He had something to explain to his sister.

* * * * * * * * * * * *

(*Teacher:* The following is suggested for use after the story as a lead for the invitation.)

It looks as if Hamid has brought little Kinza to the right place, doesn't it? Surely now he will find out about the Lord Jesus, who loves young children and wants to make them safe forever. Surely now Hamid will learn that he need not be afraid of darkness–not if he trusts in the Lord Jesus.

All of this we shall find out later on in our story. But *we* *ourselves* need to know the Lord Jesus Christ as *our* Saviour. Perhaps, you, too, are afraid of darkness. You need not be. You can take the Lord Jesus as your Saviour this very day, if you will.

Chapter 3

The *aim* of the lesson: Contrast the "darkness of sin" with the "Light of the world," showing the redemption God has provided so that we may have "no darkness at all."

Teacher, Did you know . . .
STREET CHILDREN

There are approximately 1,000 street children in Casablanca alone (one of Morocco's cities). Street children are kids who have run away from abusive parents; have been abandoned by their poor, large families; or have been orphaned and have no relatives to care for them. Street children often become involved in gangs just to survive. They look for jobs at kiosks to earn money (e.g., cooking donuts like Hamid did, washing dishes for a restaurant, polishing shoes, etc.). Some street children live on the streets, in underpasses, in abandoned railroad cars, or in cardboard boxes. They sometimes get money for food by breaking into cars or shops. The missionary nurse in *No Darkness at All* offered the street children a meal each day, treated their medical problems, and shared the love of Jesus with them.

Kinza did not like being awakened, and she did not like the smell of the rubbish heap she was sitting on. She was getting ready to cry. Hamid was afraid she would be heard by passersby. "No, no, little sister," he said. "You must not cry. Soon you are going to be nice and warm and happy. Listen carefully now to what I tell you. I am going to put you down by yourself. You must keep very still and you must not cry. If you cry, a lady will come and beat you–hard. If you do not cry, she will come and give you a nice sweet."

This Kinza understood. She knew only too well what it meant to be beaten, and she was very hungry. If Hamid said she would get something to eat by keeping still and not crying, she would surely try.

Hamid straightened out the dirty little dress and the matted curls as best he could. Then, lifting her very gently, he carried her to the door of the Christian nurse's house. He peeked inside the slightly open door once more and looked longingly at the picture of the Lord Jesus and the children.

Show Illustration #18

To Hamid it seemed the eyes of the Lord Jesus were looking lovingly, straight at him and little Kinza.

What are the boys inside chanting? Hamid wondered. It did not sound like a lesson from the Qur'an (Muslim sacred scriptures). Yet the boys chanted in the same even rhythm they used when they studied in Muslim schools.

Show Memory Poster 2

(*Teacher:* Repeat as a chant: Jesus said, "I am the Light of the world: he that followeth Me shall

Then spake Jesus again unto them, saying, "I am the Light of the world; he that followeth Me shall not walk in darkness, but shall have the Light of life." John 8:12

not walk in darkness, but shall have the Light of life.") The young voices repeated the words over and over again. Hamid found himself saying the words softly with them, tucking them away in his memory to think about later.

Hamid put his last crust of bread in little Kinza's hand, placed her on the floor and whispered, "Good-bye, little sister. Remember what I have told you," and hurried away to hide in the dark alley, tears in his eyes and an awful tightness in his throat. *I shall never see my little sister again,* he thought. *Never!*

Show Illustration #19

Sitting there in the darkness he hated so much, Hamid thought again of the words he had heard, "I am the Light of the world." Hamid knew about moonlight and starlight. He knew about sunlight, candlelight, and the glare of the lights in the streets of the city. But of the "Light of the world" he knew nothing.

How wonderful it would be never again to have to walk in darkness! Hamid shuddered as he thought of the dark nights he had fought through with Kinza on his back. He thought of the terrible fear then, and now, which made his heart feel so tight.

Soon Hamid heard the boys coming out of the Christian nurse's house. He peeked out of the alley and listened to what they were saying. They were all talking about a little girl the nurse had found sitting inside her door. "Where do you suppose she could have come from?" they were asking.

After the boys were out of sight, Hamid crept out of the alley again and back to the rubbish heaHe saw the door to the nurse's house was now fast shut. But he saw a light in an upper window. Hamid crossed the street where he could watch the light coming from that upper window. *How good light is,* he thought. In their chant the boys had said, "Shall not walk in darkness." It would be so good never to walk in darkness–to have *no darkness at all.*

Show Illustration #20

As Hamid kept his eyes on the window, he saw the figure of a woman pass by. She was carrying a child in her arms. The child did not struggle nor seem afraid. Instead Hamid saw a little hand reach up to feel the face of the woman. He knew it was Kinza who was "seeing" with her hands.

Back to the rubbish heap Hamid went. He did not know where else to go. He covered himself as best he could with his rags and, using his arm for a pillow, went to sleep–a very tired, very hungry, very lonely boy who dreamed he saw Kinza being held safely and lovingly in the arms of the Man in the picture.

When Hamid awoke the next morning he was stiff and cold. His first thoughts were of Kinza. But he was hungry. So he wandered along the streets through the deserted marketplace, hoping to find food.

Soon the town began to wake uMerchants began taking down the shutters from their shop windows. As Hamid stood watching, suddenly his nose told him something good to eat was nearby.

Turning, Hamid discovered he had been standing close to a little stall where a man was frying dough rings in hot oil. Hamid was so hungry his stomach seemed to flip right over as he watched the man string the delicious-smelling little doughnuts on strong blades of grass (reeds) for his customers. The man kept muttering and scolding because he had to stop his work from time to time to blow up the fire under the stone pot.

Boldly Hamid stepped forward. "Do you need an assistant, Sir?"

The man looked carefully at Hamid. Seeming to be satisfied he said, "Take the bellows and blow up the fire, and if I find you helping yourself to anything that doesn't belong to you, the police station is right over there." The man pointed with a greasy finger.

Show Illustration #21

Poor Hamid sat down and began to blow up the fire with the bellows. It was hot, and he felt very weak. But he was determined to earn a breakfast, so he kept on. His master's voice seemed to come from a great distance: "Enough! Now stand here and thread these dough rings on the reeds."

Hamid had been working about two hours when the man suddenly asked, "Have you had any breakfast?"

"No, Sir. And no supper last night."

Show Illustration #22

As Hamid began hungrily to eat the dough rings the man had given him, he noticed a group of boys eyeing him. The boys were sitting on the cobblestones. They were, Hamid decided, about his own age. They, too, were hungry.

The doughnut shop was closed in the middle of the morning. Hamid had worked so well, the master told him as he handed him a small piece of money, that he might return the next morning.

As Hamid turned to leave, the group of boys got to their feet and followed him. One of them spoke. He asked Hamid where he had come from, why he was there, where his mother and father were, and where he lived.

You may be sure Hamid was very careful how he answered. He told the boy he had come from the country to find work, that his mother and father were dead, and that he lived in the streets.

"We, too, live in the streets," his companion said. "If you would like to be one of us, buy a loaf of bread with that money, and share it with us. If you do, we will show you where we go for supper at night."

Hamid bought his loaf quickly and spent the change on a handful of bitter black olives. Sitting under a eucalyptus tree, he shared the food with the gang of boys.

* * * * * * * * * * * *

Hamid might have guessed that the boys (with whom he had shared his food) were speaking of the nurse's home, when they said they would show him where they got their supper at night. Yet he was surprised when they turned to go in the open door at which he had left Kinza the night before.

Thinking that the nurse might refuse to shelter Kinza if she knew Hamid was her brother, he was afraid to go inside. Yet the light, the warmth, and the smell of delicious food were more than the hungry boy could resist. *If I do not speak,* he thought, *Kinza will not know I am there. Besides, I'd like to see her.*

And so it was that Hamid was among the boys who went each night to eat and to hear the Word of God. The nurse noticed, and spoke kindly to Hamid. His heart felt so good, not "tight" any more. Here was light. Here was kindness. Here was food. And here was Kinza, sweet and clean and content. What more could a boy want?

Perhaps Hamid *thought* he wanted nothing more. But, oh, how much more he needed!

Show Illustration #23

He began to realize this, as the nurse spoke of the Man in the picture who loved boys and girls, and indeed everyone in the world. She told them how this Man, the Lord Jesus Christ, had left Heaven where He was very rich, and had come down to earth, where He became very poor. She said, "The Lord Jesus lived in Heaven where there is no darkness at all. Yet He came to earth and took the punishment for our sins by dying on the cross. He did it to redeem us . . . to buy us for Himself."

Hamid thought about his stepfather's plans to sell Kinza to the old beggar. *If I could have paid a higher price than the beggar, I would have bought Kinza for myself,* Hamid thought.

"The Lord Jesus could buy us for Himself," the nurse continued, "because He is the perfect Son of God. He gave His perfect life for us. No one could pay a higher price than that. He did this because He loves us so much. Now, when we trust Him to forgive our sins and ask Him to become our Saviour, He saves us from darkness forever. He promises that someday we shall also live with Him in Heaven, where He has gone to prepare a place for each one who will trust Him."

Hamid listened, never taking his eyes from the nurse's face, except to look occasionally at the picture. His young heart began to yearn to have the Lord Jesus as his own Saviour.

The Holy Spirit who comes to live in the hearts of Christians when they accept the Lord Jesus made the nurse see that this boy was longing to become a Christian. And so, as the boys left, she persuaded Hamid to stay a little longer. She laid her hand firmly on his shoulder and hung on to his dirty rags, for she saw that he was afraid and knew he might dash off after the other boys unless she held him.

Soon, however, as Hamid listened to her gentle voice, he lost his fright and began to talk.

Show Illustration #24

Kinza, who had been sitting quietly in her little corner, suddenly stood up and, holding her hands before her, made her way to the voice she remembered. She put her thin arms around Hamid's neck. He pressed her close to himself.

It was then the nurse saw the marked resemblance between the two. "She is your little sister, isn't she, Hamid?" the gentle voice inquired. "Do not be afraid to tell me. I shall not turn her out if she has no one to care for her."

Then the story came out. Hamid felt as though his heart were many times lighter after he had told about Kinza and was assured that she would remain with the nurse.

"It is quite late, Hamid," the nurse said. "Your friends are probably already asleep in the mosque, and you will not be able to find them. Stay here tonight. I want to talk to you some more after I have put Kinza to bed."

When Hamid was left alone in the clean tidy room, he looked around more carefully than he had done before. On a low table he noticed a bowl of eggs.

Show Illustration #25

Following his first instinct, Hamid reached out grimy hands and took two. Hiding them under his rags he sat down and waited for the nurse to return.

"Come over here, Hamid, closer to the light," the nurse said when she returned. "It is more pleasant than that dark corner."

"I'd rather sit here," was all that Hamid said.

It was all he needed to say in order for the nurse to know that all was not well. She knew that Muslim children hate darkness and are afraid of it.

Walking over to Hamid she made him stand. "Lift your arms," she said in a firm voice. When Hamid refused, she tried to reach under his rags. As she did so she squashed the eggs. What a mess poor Hamid was now!

After a bath and some clean clothing, the nurse spoke kindly to the trembling boy.

"Hamid," she said, "you were afraid to come and sit in the light because of your sin. Those were my eggs and you stole them. You deserve to be punished. But they were my eggs. I paid for them. And I am going to forgive you. I love you, Hamid, and I want you to come here. But you must promise never to steal anything from my house again."

Hamid nodded. It was the first time he had ever been sorry for his stealing–except to be sorry that he had been caught! "And remember," the nurse said, "sin and darkness go together. But the Lord Jesus is the Light of the world. He loves you and wants you to walk with Him in the light. He died to buy you–redeem you–for Himself. He wants you to live with Him in a wonderful place called Heaven, where there is no darkness at all.

"But now, Hamid, you must tell Him of your sins, and ask Him to wash away its stains and make you clean just as I washed away all the broken eggs."

For the first time since he was a baby, Hamid was crying. He did not seem to be ashamed, as he had been taught to think of tears. He was ready indeed to do as the kind nurse had said. How wonderful that the Lord Jesus could buy him for Himself!

"Do you believe that the Lord Jesus is the Son of God? Do you believe He died on the cross for you? Will you put your trust in Him and receive Him as your Saviour? Do you want to kneel and ask God to forgive you for Jesus' sake?"

"Yes! Yes!"

And so it was that late on a dark night in Morocco, a Muslim boy opened his heart, and the light of the love of God in Christ Jesus came in. Hamid became a child of God.

Hamid learned that his debt of sin was paid, and that the Lord Jesus had bought (redeemed) him for Himself. Do you know that the debt has been paid for *your* sin? Have you accepted Him as the payment for your debt? Believe Him. Receive Him. Thank Him for being your Redeemer–for making you His own.

Chapter 4

The *aim* of the lesson: Contrast the "darkness of sin" with the "Light of the world," showing the redemption God has provided so that we may have "no darkness at all." There is no difference between the refined and respectable, like Jenny–and the poor and uncouth, like Hamid. Both are as much in need of the Saviour.

Far away from the place where Hamid came to know the Lord Jesus as the Light of the world, and where little blind Kinza found loving care, there lived a girl who was also living in darkness.

Show Illustration #26

Jenny, living in a home of wealth in England, would have been surprised and angry if she had heard any person say that she was living in darkness. But she really was. For, you see, Jenny had never taken the Lord Jesus as her Saviour.

Jenny was worse off than little blind Kinza who was blind physically. Jenny was much worse off than Hamid, who was pitifully poor. He had almost nothing at all. But Hamid had the Light of life–the Lord Jesus Christ. Hamid was not in darkness any more. But Jenny was, in spite of all the wonderful things her parents gave her.

But there was someone praying for Jenny. It was the Christian nurse in faraway Morocco. The nurse was Jenny's aunt.

I am sure neither Jenny nor her parents realized it was an answer to prayer when Jenny got sick right after Christmas. The doctor said that nine-year-old Jenny must get away from the cold, damp weather of England. It was then that Jenny's parents remembered there was almost constant sunshine in Morocco, where Jenny's aunt was a missionary.

"Let's take Jenny to Morocco for a visit," her father said one day. And before very long they were off!

Jenny and her parents sailed across the channel from England to France, taking their automobile on the ferry with them. Then they drove south through France and Spain, crossed a narrow channel again–and there they were, in Morocco.

Jenny was happy and excited to be going to a strange land, and to be going to visit the aunt she loved very much. During most of the trip she played with her new toys and sang Christmas carols, remembering the wonderful Christmas music she enjoyed so much. She sang most often the carol which ended, "Guide me to Thy perfect Light." Jenny did not have the tiniest idea that this was exactly what God was doing for her, in answer to her aunt's prayers.

Show Illustration #27

When Jenny and her parents arrived at the hotel where they were to stay in Morocco, they found many dirty little boys crowding around their shiny car. The boys fought each other for a chance to carry the luggage and earn a few cents.

Jenny was kept inside the car until all the luggage was away and the dirty boys had left. When she saw her aunt, she also saw little Kinza standing beside the nurse. "Why, Auntie, you never told us you had a little girl," Jenny squealed. "This is wonderful! Isn't she darling, Mother?"

As Jenny stood beside Kinza, many passersby stopped to look at the English girl with the long blonde hair and blue eyes. Jenny looked lovely and clean in her blue dress. The passersby looked down in wonder at her white shoes. They also noticed how very fair her skin was.

Show Illustration #28

But Jenny saw none of this. She was trying to get Kinza to make friends with her by offering her one of her dolls. Of course Kinza paid no attention.

"What's the matter with your little girl, Auntie?" Jenny pouted. "I am sure she doesn't have lots of nice toys like I have. But she won't even reach out and take this new doll. Of course, if she doesn't appreciate what I want to do for her, I'll just keep it myself." And Jenny started to walk away from Kinza.

The nurse took hold of Jenny's hand. "Let me show you," she said. But Jenny, spoiled child that she was, pulled away. Then the nurse said, "Jenny, Kinza is blind. She could not see your doll."

"Well, you might have told me sooner," Jenny pouted.

Jenny's aunt looked at her niece. "Dear God," she prayed silently, "please let Jenny come to the Light and receive the Lord Jesus as her Saviour before she leaves here. Please show me how to talk to her."

After Jenny and her parents had settled their belongings in the hotel and put on clean clothing, they walked over to the nurse's home.

Show Illustration #29

Jenny turned up her little tip-tilted nose when she saw the ragged beggars and dirty babies sitting on the cobblestones. And when she saw her aunt putting a key in the door of one of the miserable houses

in a narrow street, she spoke right out, "Auntie, don't tell me this is where you live! How awful!"

But Jenny forgot about her dislike of the poverty and filth she saw around her when her aunt allowed her to help care for a tiny sick baby. "There is nothing she can 'catch,'" the nurse assured Jenny's parents when they objected.

"Even if there is, I want to help, and I am *going* to helThat is all there is to it!" Jenny exclaimed.

Jenny did not realize it–for she did not yet know Hamid– that she was just as much a sinner as Hamid had been. Hamid lied and stole. But Jenny was willful and selfish. She was as much in darkness as Hamid.

Show Illustration #30

Jenny hurried to get a cup and spoon and some sugar as her aunt told her to do. Then she ran and got the kettle, and found the white cubes on the third shelf. All this she did quickly, even though she was in a strange house. Jenny did not like the way her aunt said, "Now, please rinse out the cup and spoon with some of that boiled water. Now crush up one cube. Mix it with a very little water. Please pass me that bottle." Jenny did not like taking orders. But she did like feeling important. When the baby seemed better, and the nurse sent the mother away, Jenny announced, "When I am grown, I shall be a missionary nurse and order everyone around and make sick babies well!"

Jenny's aunt looked at her niece. "You couldn't be a missionary unless something very important happened to you first, Jenny."

"What important thing, besides learning to be a nurse?" Jenny wanted to know.

"Let us talk about that later," her auntie said. "Right now, I have neglected you and your mother and father long enough. I must get something ready to eat. You must be very hungry."

Jenny thought, *Whatever else it is I need to know, I am certain I could learn it. I am the smartest girl in my class, and the richest. My father and mother will give me anything I want.*

Show Illustration #31

Some days later the nurse took her niece and Kinza for a little picnic in a beautiful garden. Kinza had her little face deep in a big bun, and Jenny was holding a sandwich when she asked, "Auntie, what else would I have to know to be a missionary nurse?"

"It depends on what you will do," her aunt replied. "If all you want to do is to make them well, then all you have to do is to train as a nurse or a doctor. But when you make them well, they get sick again soon, for they do not have enough to eat and they do not know how to keep well. Most of them will die quite young anyhow. Their bodies do not usually last very long."

"Then why bother with them?" Jenny demanded, tossing her head.

"The part of each child that really matters is the part that lasts forever," her aunt replied. "It is the child's *real* self. We call it the spirit. The only way you can help them and make them *really* happy is by leading them to the Lord Jesus. But, Jenny, you cannot possibly show the Lord Jesus to anyone unless you know Him yourself. So, you see, it isn't *what* you know, as much as *Whom* you know."

Jenny looked surprised. For once she could find nothing to say in reply to her aunt.

"You see, Jenny," her aunt continued, "these people are afraid of death. To them it means nothing but darkness. And so they come to me for medicine. I give them medicine. But I give them much more. I also tell them about the Lord Jesus who died that they might have eternal life and light. I give the medicine because I want them to see that the Lord Jesus, in me, cares about their pain and wants to help them. It's no good *talking* about love. They do not understand love. But I *show* them what love is by doing loving deeds."

Jenny squirmed as her aunt added, "The first thing you have to do before becoming a missionary nurse is to be sure that the Lord Jesus is actually in your heart, loving the poor people *through* you. Otherwise it's just like taking an empty lantern out in the dark."

Jenny sat silent for a moment. Then she said, "Auntie, how do you know if He is in your heart or not?"

"How does the light get into the empty lantern?"

Show Illustration #32

"Someone puts a candle inside and then lights it," Jenny answered.

"That is correct, dear. But remember, the first thing we must do is to open our heart's door and ask the Lord Jesus to come in and to cleanse us from our sin, believing that He died for us."

"But, Auntie, I don't think I have any sin to be 'cleansed.'"

Drawing the little girl into her arms the nurse whispered, "Jenny, dear, you were not here five minutes before I knew you were a sinner."

Jenny pulled away and looked at her aunt, half in anger and half in surprise. "Me, a sinner?" she exclaimed. "I've always been a good girl. My mother says so."

"But God says, 'All have sinned and come short of the glory of God,' Jenny. When you think of how good and perfect the Lord Jesus is, you will realize that being stubborn, and willful, and selfish, is great sin in God's sight. These things I have seen in you, Jenny. Remember, none but the Lord Jesus has ever been good enough to get to Heaven. Because He is perfect, He is able to cleanse us."

But Jenny had heard enough. Her stubborn little heart was not willing to admit she was a sinner, needing to be made clean.

Jumping to her feet, she exclaimed, "I'd better go after Kinza. She might get lost. And then I think we'd better get back. My parents will be looking for me."

With a sad heart the nurse gathered the picnic things and took the girls home, praying as she walked, "Please, Father, may Jenny yield to You soon."

Jenny did not like what her aunt had said. She had always been the most important person in her little world. Why, every child in school knew it was an honor to be invited to Jenny's house. She was no sinner!

But that night, when Jenny went to bed, she was a troubled girl who could not slee Finally she crawled out of bed and got dressed. She went to find her mother and father in the hotel lobby. "I want to go to Auntie's home right now," she announced. "You take me. Then leave me there. I have to talk to her tonight. She will bring me home." When she saw her father look as though he were going to say "no" for sure, Jenny's eyes filled with tears and she added, "Please?"

Jenny's aunt was surprised to see her niece at night. But she knew at once what was troubling the girl. She said nothing until Jenny began the conversation.

Show Illustration #33

"Auntie, what did you mean when you said that the Lord Jesus can cleanse us? I have to know."

Jenny's aunt sat close to her willful niece as she held up a little book of colors. She used this to explain that every person is born with a sinful heart. (*Teacher:* Show *Wordless Book*, turning very briefly to the dark page when speaking of sin, to the red page when speaking of the death of Christ, and to the white page when speaking of forgiveness. Save detailed explanation until after this story. To tell it at this point makes the story too long.)

"You are not a sinner because you are sometimes mean and selfish, Jenny. You are mean and selfish because you *are* a sinner. We cannot help ourselves. We need Someone to come into our lives and forgive our sin. The Lord Jesus is the only One who can do this. Because He is not a sinner, He could take your place and die for you. This makes it possible for your sin to be forgiven. But we must *accept* His offer of forgiveness just the same as we accept a gift. We do not pay for it. We cannot pay for our salvation, for it costs too much. We *can* believe in the Lord Jesus and accept His gift of salvation. That is all He asks us to do. We confess our sins to Him and ask Him to come into our heart and life. He gives us His light, instead of our darkness. When we do this, we understand what He means when He says, 'I am the Light of the world: he that followeth Me shall not walk in darkness, but shall have the Light of life.'" (John 8:12)

Show Memory Verse Poster 2

"I want the Lord Jesus' light in my heart, instead of my darkness," Jenny cried. "I want His light to shine out of my heart so I can help others. Will He truly come in if I ask Him, Auntie?"

"He will if you truly believe and trust Him fully, little niece."

"Oh, I do! I do! Auntie, I truly do!"

And then, away off in the dark land of Morocco, while little Kinza slept peacefully in her clean bed close by, Jenny, the rich girl from England, came out of the kingdom of darkness where Satan rules, to the kingdom of light, where God rules.

Chapter 5

The *aim* of the lesson: To show that devotion to and love for the Lord results in witnessing for Him.

Hamid went every day to the nurse's house. He wanted to learn to read the Bible that she had given him. And he was learning very quickly–as anyone does when he really has a desire to learn.

Hamid was entirely happy until the man and woman with their little girl came from England to visit. He felt that the young girl, who called his beloved nurse "Auntie," might be taking his place. Then, when he saw how kind the three visitors were to Kinza, he was sorry for being jealous. He would just wait until they went home again. Then he would go back for more reading lessons.

One morning as Hamid was working at his usual job of blowing up the fire and stringing doughnuts on reeds, he looked across the street and saw something that made his young heart almost stop beating.

Show Illustration #34

That man was surely his stepfather! And the man was watching the nurse, with her grown-up visitors, walk down the street toward him. With them was the little girl from England–and Kinza. Hamid ducked down behind the counter.

As he worked with the fire, he wondered what he ought to do. His first thought was to get away from there as quickly as possible. Kinza, he felt, was safe with all her newfound friends. As much as he might wish to, his stepfather would not be able to grab Kinza away from them. They all loved her, and one or the other would always watch her. But he, Hamid, was not safe. His stepfather, he knew, would grab him, beat him, and make him steal Kinza away from the nurse's house. Yes, the best thing for him to do was to run away as fast as he could. And without a word to his master, Hamid scurried away–down the street, around the corner, and to the hills.

Hamid hid all night long in the hills and intended to stay there a day or two longer. But the next morning he heard the voice of his beloved nurse calling, "Hamid! Hamid! If you are here anywhere, please come to me. We are in trouble, Hamid! Please come to me. One of your friends said he saw you run up here."

Show Illustration #35

Hamid could not stay hidden when the nurse called to him so pleadingly: suddenly there he was before her eyes. The nurse was startled. "I shall never get accustomed to the way you boys of Morocco disappear and appear as though from nowhere!" she exclaimed.

"You are in trouble?"

"Yes, Hamid. We *are* in trouble. Kinza has disappeared and we cannot find her anywhere. We left her with my niece for only a very few moments while her parents and I bought something in the market. And, just as you seem to be able to disappear and appear so suddenly, Kinza was gone! My niece said she thought she was watching her every moment. But suddenly she was gone."

Trembling, Hamid said, "My stepfather has taken her away."

"Why do you say that, Hamid?"

"I saw him in the marketplace yesterday as I worked in the doughnut shoHe was watching you and your friends walk down the street. I saw him watching Kinza and knew he wanted to steal her away and sell her to the beggar. But I never thought you would leave her alone with that girl from England."

Gently the nurse said, "Hamid, I did not know she was in danger. You did know. And yet you ran away to save yourself. We both did wrong, Hamid. Now we must try to get her back."

"That would be impossible." Hamid sighed.

"But I have a plan," the nurse said. "I am sure my visitors would drive their car to your old home. I would make them give me Kinza."

"But you do not know the way to the village," Hamid cried.

"You will go with us and show us the way."

Hamid lifted frightened eyes to the nurse's face. "Do you know what they will do to me if I take you there?" he asked.

"But they shall not catch you, Hamid. You will only point out your house to us. We will do the rest."

Show Illustration #36

That very morning Hamid's friends watched as he rode off in the shiny English automobile. How they envied him! Hamid smiled and waved to them. He would not let them see how frightened he was. It was a beautiful drive. Hamid remembered the hot, dusty evening when he had climbed the hill with Kinza on his back.

Hamid grew less frightened as the big man and the nurse kept assuring him that they would allow no harm to come to him. But his heart was sad when he thought of his mother. He would be very close to her, and he longed to see her. Then, just as darkness began to fall, Hamid saw the shape of his home village with the thatched-roof huts.

They had to leave the car in the marketplace of the village, for the path was too narrow for a car. Hamid ducked out of sight when he saw anyone he thought might recognize him, as he led the Englishman and the nurse along the path to his old home. They were close enough for Hamid to see his own lamp-lit doorway and the glow of the charcoal fire. "There," he whispered, "it is the third house beyond the fig tree."

"We'll meet you at the car," the nurse said. And she was gone. Then Hamid hid. He thought of the Light which was now within him and of how wonderful it was not to be afraid of the darkness now. Nor did he need to be afraid of so-called evil spirits, as he once was.

Creeping silently, closer to the hut, Hamid listened and peeked inside from time to time.

Show Illustration #37

He saw his stepfather rise to greet the visitors, and heard the sound of hurrying about inside the hut. Then he heard the nurse say, "I've come to find out about your little blind girl, Kinza. She was left in my charge by her brother about seven months ago. I wish very much to have her back. She is your child, and it must be as you say. But I am willing to pay a higher price for her than another would give to you."

The stepfather spread out his hands, palms upward. "But I know nothing of the child," he said. "True, her brother stole her away seven months ago. But I have neither seen nor heard of her since. If I hear news of her I will gladly bring her to you."

Peeking through the low doorway Hamid could see his mother sitting on the other side of the fire. He saw her look hard at the nurse in the way he remembered when she wanted to tell something and did not dare speak. As the nurse watched, Hamid saw his mother give a faint nod in the direction of the old wife.

That look and slight nod were enough for the nurse. She noticed a blanket behind the old woman, and saw that a little girl's face was peeking out. Hamid shook as he saw her walk toward the blanket, then he suddenly called out, "Kinza! Kinza!"

The stepfather stood–pale with fright. The old woman clutched at the blanket. But she was too late.

Show Illustration #38

Recognizing the voice of the one she had come to love so much, Kinza sprang up with a loud, glad cry and crawled out from under the blanket.

The nurse lifted the blanket to help free Kinza and soon she was holding the child in her arms. She then turned to face the stepfather.

The stepfather was angry! The Englishman stepped up beside the nurse. He was a big man, and the stepfather knew it would be best to let them have Kinza, if they were willing to pay a good price. When Hamid saw what had happened, he hurried away as fast as he could to the car.

As Hamid hid beside the car he heard a voice he loved calling him softly, "Hamid! Hamid, my son!"

Show Illustration #39

Hamid slid out from behind the car and kissed his mother's hand. She drew him back into the shadow.

"Little son, little son," she whispered. "Are you well? I am so glad you were able to take your little sister to this good woman. Keep watch over her, Hamid, for your stepfather will surely try to steal her again."

Then Hamid told his mother how he had found the picture and, better yet, had learned to know the Man of the picture–the Lord Jesus–Who is alive and in Heaven. He told her how the nurse was teaching him about God's Book, the Bible. "I must learn more and more," he said.

Hamid's mother drew him close to her. "Then you must come and tell me, my son, that my heart may be happy, also." Hamid rested his head against his mother's shoulder. He wanted to stay with her.

"I will go back now," he whispered, "and I'll learn better how to read from the Book that tells the way to Heaven. Then when the harvest is ripe, I'll come home and tell you all about it."

Steps sounded on the pathway, and the rays of a flashlight beamed on them. They quickly stepped out of the light. Hamid's mother stooped and kissed Kinza, whispered a blessing on the nurse, and gave her hand to her son. Then she was vanished up the path–and to the punishment she knew awaited her.

Just as they were about to get into the car, the angry stepfather raced toward them. "You may have the child," he shouted, "but my son, Hamid, you may not have. I know he must be here."

The Englishman jumped into the driver's seat and turned on the motor, as Hamid, the nurse, and Kinza all fell inside. The car raced away with a roar, bouncing them around inside like cattle. But who cared? They were safely away from the wicked stepfather. And Kinza was with them!

Hamid rested his arms then on the back window ledge and looked back at the village where he had lived, and where the name of Jesus Christ had never been breathed, as far as he knew. Somehow, the boy knew that one day he would come back, alone and on foot. He would not be afraid, for the Light within him would make him brave. He repeated softly, "Jesus said, 'I am the Light of the world; he that followeth Me shall not walk in darkness, but shall have the Light of life!'"

You may be sure the missionary nurse kept better watch over Kinza after that. She knew the stepfather would surely try to get more money for the little blind girl by stealing her again and selling her to the beggar.

Hamid's heart was sad one day when he heard his nurse talking to her visitors before they left to return to England. "Yes, I know it would be best for her," she said. "You can take her to the school for blind children where she will learn to read. Yet, she dare not go unless you promise to teach her about the Lord Jesus and give her an opportunity to receive Him as her Saviour. Without Him she is blind spiritually. And that is far worse than being blind physically."

Hamid knew the nurse was doing the best thing for Kinza when, after receiving the promise she demanded, she allowed Kinza to go to England with her niece and the parents.

Show Illustration #40

He stood beside the nurse as they drove off. For the second time in his young life he allowed the tears to run down his cheeks and was not ashamed. He waved as long as he could see the car, then turned with the nurse to go back up the long narrow street. "My little sister will never need me again," Hamid said.

The nurse took Hamid home with her. "Would you like to come and live with me?" she asked. "You could take Kinza's place and be my boy."

Hamid thought long and hard, then shook his head slowly. "It would be very pleasant," he said, "but I should never be able to get my friends to accept the Lord Jesus if I did not live as they live."

Hamid had a faraway look in his eyes as he thought of returning to his village. "I want to learn to read well enough by harvest time so that I shall be able to return home and try to teach my mother, and all who will listen. I cannot stay and enjoy the life I would have with you, knowing that they are still in darkness."

The nurse pressed Hamid's hands to her cheek, as she had seen his mother do. "Now, Hamid, I know that surely you have the Light of the world in your heart, for you wish others to know the Lord Jesus as you do. That, Hamid, is why I left my home and country to come here to Morocco. It was God's love in my heart which gave me the love and desire to tell others. That love He has also given to you, Hamid. Did you know the Lord Jesus once said, 'Go ye into all the world and preach the Gospel'? That is what we are both doing now."

The nurse's words were never forgotten. They helped Hamid to take that long, dusty path to his home one day, just as he had planned.

Show Illustration #41

Waving to the nurse as he left, Hamid went, not afraid now of the darkness, nor of the beatings he was sure to receive. There was gladness in his heart and love: Love for the Lord Jesus who had died that he might be free. Love for those who knew not the Lord Jesus.

The nurse watched, tears in her eyes, as the young missionary set out.

What about you? Will you, like Hamid, go and tell others about the Light of the world?

If the children want to know–yes, indeed, Kinza later received the Lord Jesus as her own Saviour!

Teacher, Did you know . . .

FAMOUS CHRISTIANS OF NORTH AFRICA

The Apostle Mark (who wrote the Gospel of Mark) is believed to have been from <u>Libya</u>, now a Muslim country.

Through evangelist Philip (Acts 8), an <u>Ethiopian</u> was saved. This conversion is believed by many to have been the beginning of the North African Coptic Church!

Tertullian lived around AD 200 in Carthage, now <u>Tunisia</u>. He was converted to Jesus after observing Christians' bravery as they were being killed for their beliefs. He was the first to defend the scriptural doctrine of the Trinity: God is three Persons yet One God. He is called the "first Protestant" because he taught that the church was not bishops, but a union of people brought together by the Holy Spirit.

Origen lived AD 185-245 in Alexandria, <u>Egypt</u>. He argued against Gnosticism (which said Jesus was less than God) as Paul did earlier in the book of Colossians. Under his leadership the 27 books of the New Testament were collected (canonized) to form the Bible. He called the Scriptures "springs of salvation." (Teacher: BVI does not necessarily agree with all the doctrines of the early church fathers.)

REACHING MUSLIMS IN CLOSED OR RESTRICTED-ACCESS COUNTRIES

There are approximately 500 Christians in Morocco (as of 2005). They meet in very small, private groups to share and pray with each other. It is estimated that 80% of Moroccans have never heard the Gospel.

Fourteen hundred years ago, the Christian church in Morocco was mostly Berber people. Arab Muslim invaders wiped out the Berber church in mid-600 (AD).

The Moroccan government did not allow Christian missions into the country until the 1960s. Only service-oriented (medical personnel, educators, etc.) Christians are allowed to live in Morocco. Morocco appears committed to the Muslim faith and the Islamic law. The government is committed to keeping Morocco a Muslim country. Converts to Christ are not allowed to conduct public church meetings. The largest denomination of Muslims in the world is the Sunni Muslims, and Morocco is mostly Sunni. They strictly follow the customs of Muhammad in the Hadith (book about the rules and regulations of being a Muslim).

Then how can a Muslim in Morocco hear the Gospel since it is a "closed" or "restricted-access" country?

1. By reading Arabic language Christian literature and/or Bibles perhaps smuggled into the country. But such literature must be read in private at great risk. For example, a Muslim woman who reads a Bible might hear her husband say "leave this home" or "I divorce you."

2. By hearing the Gospel through Christians working as medical workers, teaching English as a second language, operating an orphanage, etc. They cautiously share the good news about Jesus and model His love.

3. By hearing the Gospel on Christian television and radio programs broadcast into Morocco via satellite.

4. By taking a Bible correspondence course received in the mail.

5. By visiting Christian Web sites on the Internet.

6. By viewing the Arabic translation of the Jesus Film.

Pray for protection for those who come to know Jesus through these various means.

Usually after Christians share the Gospel with Muslims over many occasions, only a few dare to leave Islam to turn to Jesus. It takes great courage because it is against Islamic law for a Muslim to become a Christian! If a person becomes a Christian, he/she can expect trouble: sometimes be cut off from his/her family, imprisoned, treated as if he/she is mentally ill, lose his or her job or even his/her life. A convert's sincerity toward Jesus is often severely tested (Mark 4:17). Hamid desired to return to his village and share the Gospel with his mother. Jesus told Christians to be ready for difficult times (John 15:18-19; 2 Timothy 3:12; and Hebrews 13:3). But He also said that troubles cannot separate Christians from His love (Romans 8:35).

Check for Arabic translation of *The Life of Christ Visualized Bible Series* on the Bible Visuals International Web site (www.biblevisuals.org).

Made in the USA
Las Vegas, NV
28 December 2022

64297922R00038